Odes

THE WILD LILY INSTITUTE

IBSN *978-1-312-31840-3*

Second Edition: First Printing 2023
Also: Illustrated edition *978-1-387-43306-3*

Cover design and interior layout: Voetelle Art & Design
Cover image: Licensed from Adobe Stock.

Published by:

 Potter's Press

a division of
The Wild Lily Institute
P.O. Box 888
Abbotsford PO A, BC
Canada
V2T 7A2

www.wildlilyinstitute.com

Odes

Emily Isaacson

Potter's Press
Vancouver

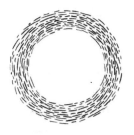

Dedicated to

Ingrid

A seed hidden in the heart of an apple is an orchard invisible.

—A Welsh proverb

Contents

Swan Lake

There was a slow glowing light
as the amber sunlight at this basted liquid hour
over the effulgent muddy foliage
of the highest Garry oak on Christmas Hill,
as a priest ordains a women's shelter
a safe place.
How when you are unable to speak,
there is the Scotch broom and chocolate lily,
an old rustle commissions the knotted leaves,
a gold flute tunes the order amid the last rays.
The red sun has risen and set with a dying cry.
Crows bellow from the Pacific crab apple:
the inner sanctum under my temples.
A knot in the trunk is a black eye of modernity,
while a deep well caverns
a crackling enameled wasp nest.
Broken ivory cranium . . . when I run
I cannot move, rooted in place,
in deep lustrous ground.
My dead fellowship branches falling
into the white brodiaea; with veins, her slender stalks run
from basal pain, but undemanding,
want perfection like a fool's onion.
I asked to be burned at the stake for my sins,
but was beautified:
how when you come around the corner
there are two street people
in the middle of the night
and one of them is naked in the rain.

Introduction

I have long wondered whether our love for trees is what drives us to buy recycled paper. There are so many facets of connection, made real and renewed every time we are in nature. The throwback to animism, where we acknowledge a higher power that has given soul to nature, and spirit to trees, endears us to them like friends. Indeed, the sacred bond between trees and people goes back to the beginning of poetry, and in essence the beginning of poetry could not exist without a tribute to trees.

These poems are selected based on the thirteen months of the Celtic Tree Calendar. Departing from all controversies regarding its authenticity, we would rise to the occasion by having new insight into the personalities of the trees chosen. We would aspire to an equal level of adeptness as to the unique characteristics, qualities, and energy that influenced the spiritual connection to each tree. The trees and botanicals in this book are heralded in the form of odes.

As a classical form, odes have been around since antiquity, and are originally used to elevate the object in a heroic way. The Romantic Movement rediscovered their poets in this form; Keats celebrated autumn and the nightingale. Contemporary poetry has imbued the decorum of the ode, and expanded its address to the equivalent of landscape photography, in their spirit of celebration.

In the nineteenth century we see from Shelley that the sonnet form is included in the structure of odes. This we also see in this volume in the Ode to a Hawthorn Tree, Ode to the Honeysuckle, Ode to the Water Lily, Ode to the Holly, Ode to the Reed and their strict Elizabethan form.

We seek out literature for inspiration to eschew control. We seek out the prophetic for protection in the spiritual realm. There is a need for visionary gifts. There is a need for seeing into the past and future with redemptive eyes. There is a yearning to stand on a hill and see all the possible tragedies that could befall any individual, and to fashion an amulet, to give hope in dark times.

This spiritual essence made from trees themselves, not just in the printing of paper, but in extracting the very oil of the tree so to speak, will ward off the dark. The extraction of the oils is one that includes no solvents, is potent, pungent, and undeniably pure. It will someday neutralize the poison of modern times, and the toxicity of our hate culture. The wounding can heal of abandonment and neglect when we are around people and nature with positive energy. The stigma of shame and abuse finds its nemesis in the blessing of the elders.

Trees can symbolize here orators, and with that meaning, they give us a sense of a voice in despair. They stand for decades if not centuries and are straight-shooting without a desire to retaliate when other best them. Trees are stalwart in beauty as they feel no need for competition. There is so much competition, that we invest in sports, but what would our family be without sibling rivalry?

Where would we be without the lovely paper birch, or how would we rise up to heaven without first lying beneath the wizened ash? How could we practice medicine without first understanding the rowan, or bury our dead without the Elegy of the Oak? We have at times had to bury our dreams. We have trod over their tombs.

I used to believe that leaves represented poetry. When the fall arrived, the many colours and textures of leaves were reminiscent of how a poem lives for awhile in us, and then falls away. Their meaning and purpose in our lives is transient. They are all around us, and paper the ground we walk on, yet we do not notice them. Leaves make us feel clothed, not self-conscious, as Adam and Eve in the Garden of Eden.

In the winters of our lives, when we have a scarce number of leaves left, let us turn to this small volume and remember the trees of our children, and the flowers of their upturned faces. We can always return here to the place of our youth and remember the cabin times we had together. The long lens of poetry brings the essentials into focus.

As for the children who grow up and go on their way: once they were young, and our spiritual connections were strong. Don't lose that precious bond to the heart of the child. Let our kindness move the tree like wind in its branches, let our warmth be like the sunlight on its leaves, and our prayers in their lives move the tree from sapwood to heartwood.

Blessings,

Emily Isaacson
The Wild Lily Institute
September 10, 2023

January

Ode to a Carnation

Your tiny face
divided into pastel sprigs
reminds me of a holiday
card . . .
speaks through a wall
in a vase,
with dimensions
on time faces,
faces on clocks,
flowers on.

Ode to a Paper Birch

The birch woman has simmered down
beneath her branches, with sunlight's last crown,
oval, slanted.
Her long hair of egg-shaped leaves
glows green
as she recites the runes
of medieval lore
from her slender curved stem. . .
Li-lo, li-lo, li-ley
she drums over the Coast Mountains.

Tall chestnut horses had
been ridden beneath her storehouse
which turns to yellow in the fall,
gold carpeting the sepia ground.

Everything she had saved over her lifetime
made up her cloak of nutrients,
of wind pollinated catkins
that have started to brown
before the seeds are eaten by deer.

Before the drawing of the day is surreal,
when even the loveless can see,
all of the wood is silent in eventide,
and the shade plays its clarinet.

Before the night wind speaks,
there is the hallowed North Star,
Polaris—
glimmering in her ethereal
white trunk
with its papery bark.

Ode to the Rowan

Where ignorance is a form
of misery,
where drawing lines leads
to broken-down doors,
we hobbled in
under the rowan tree,
we clutched our crutches.

There was a message in verse:
written into the wood,
it heartwood rang, centered
like an incantation.

'Little Red One'
you might be bitter in a papyrus hood,
in a trying universe
where everyone is nude.

In the paper made from your wood,
under your wild red berries
I will teach you again. . .
be the healer of unbreakable threads,
black, blue, white,
as if broken,
be the balm of unbearable pain.

There is one last wound
to bandage,
work is languid at five,
and blood flows.

As for the wounded,
opium
of the scarlet poppy,
but germinate when the ground
is bare of the battleground,
here the milky syrup
of the lacey bloom
and its dissected leaves
live until their zenith
in early summer,
buds nodding;
but sleep in
their red peace.

Serve the medicine.

February

Idyll of the Iris

The nacreous, mother-of-pearl cloud
between sunset and sunrise bid
the clay lie beneath the earth,
not yet formed on a potter's wheel,
illusive, waiting for a cup, a bowl, a vase,
to procure out of its shapeless form.
Yet healing emanates
where lack of dying dwells.

The bonny swan rise o'er the calm
pond swells, and iris stands straight—
a less than mediocre gate—its tear
shaped bud, from heaven descended.
Its brilliant hue, a door by which
we entered.
A woman in her fragile form
became purple iris of the morn.

Dreamscape Gray (Ode to the Ash)

Handsome, my sepulchral lot,
to lie within a churchyard plot,
to close my eyes in morbid air,
there is nothing I take with me there—
beneath the old ash tree.

My eyelids are now sealed forever,
no more to flutter—just encounter—
spirits of a better kind,
sojourned to my pallid mind.

I have died from sea to sea,
where I cried with morning's icy throng
and evening's tea.

There was a tear
that fell into my cup;
no more to handle,
I have lived enough.

March

Ode to the Apple Blossom

Pale frosted glass decree
was both innocuous and wise;
and twig-like floral mantle
hung down, decorous,
to Victorian ground.

The apple blossoms sprinkled
pouring cream with applesauce
and homespun airy cotton quilting,
deftly stitched,
in moonlit minuet.

I saw the tree like a gallows,
its arms rising into the sky,
its trunk gnarled with years
and it breathed of lower life
where dreams were trod.

Where apples would usually fall,
where whitened crook
led sheep to drink
on pastures clean and high in dew,
the shepherdess rested.

A multitude of blooms,
effulgent and with pink power,
their piercing music
and feathered grail
tells of each one.

Illumined in laser-like sincerity,
the light will dance
from moon, to ray, to ground,
through snowy branches twined
with night.

Ode to the Alder

There came a morning
(light shone through the black alders)
beyond the night of pain
in the Old World,
token in its glory,
when all the things you are not
would fall away,
oily,
and there would be nothing left
for them to torture
or make into cabinets.

Simple and serrated,
highly ornamental
with stalked winter buds,
my dark cones,
and my rabbit skins are left
for their coats, their muffs,
but rabbit no longer suffices.

Have you eaten human flesh?
In torment of me;
have you tasted of me,
breaking, aching,
low, slow,
command, demand.

I took the camphor, I drank the oil,
I am glossy when mature.
I have turned blue as sapphire.
Have you conjured up a medicine
to rival mine?
Would you give it to me by mouth?

Would you sit under an alder tree
until it turns to slow decay,
catkins floating on the breeze?
How like kin.
You are too kind.

Perhaps
I am only
conelike structures that will remain
on the branches
after the small winged nutlets
are released.

April

Clearbrook (Ode to a Daisy)

She stood in the kitchen barefoot
with mildew up to her waist
turning her white dress green
where the daisy met the stem.

She was holding the baby,
with a flowered apron,
and it spoke of the love
like a daisy chain in the grass.

She turned on the faucet,
she spilled soap
and liquid ran out
like glass between her fingers.

There was a vase of flowers
on the table,
the kind that grow wild in a field,
daisies with purple edges.

Butter dissolved into the beans,
while the family ate
roast beef,
before the truth could be arrested

dwindling
relationship dissipating
even the though the water was wine,
and their blood was war.

Ode to the Willow Tree

I arose from the sitz
baths of pain
with a remedy
from white willow bark,
hiding hurt beneath
my variegated leaves,

with the flight of wild swans
landing on hard waters
ending with the brusque clap
of their wings,

feathers brush
my stone face
without reason,
noting my myriad lives,

the floundering
trains of a green dress
of the willow, traipsing over the pond
as if it were a synagogue.

We were almost covering
for sentiment
with rough bark,
sallows' twisting trunk
standing up to hard times,
osiers from moist soil.

There was a brittle
Buddhist-like compassion
emanating from the flexibility
of a statue made
of willow tree
in obstinate colour.

May

Alegrias Audition

(Ode to the Geranium)

A salida . . .
I promised you a future in May—
I noticed you in a red dress,
evoking passion and energy,
we witnessed your exhilarating art
of sainetes
and temperament,
expanding the repertoire.

A flamenco geranium
with tocadores
supporting their guitars,
tilting their necks,
engraved.

Blood-red cells that hum in rhythm,
green arms that trill an ambiance,
eyes that pierce in poetry,
legs that dance in Andalusian,
with a fusion of influences
from folklore and opera,
whose custom mouth hits the high notes.

After all these years, still singing,
still winging it with your sheet music:
your eyes, human,
your heart, fluttering with stage fright,
with a rose in your mouth.

Ode to a Hawthorn Tree

What I forgot, you promised inward me—
where the space was that I alone create,
so as alone to prune the Hawthorn tree,
so as to speak and clear enunciate.
Where I green lived, I waited silently—
cut off from noise, and sound, and dark music
abruptly, from austere humanity—
treed web, whitethorn, roses deep, violet
in berry spinning, apple of a note:
where I live in bitter pain and drink gall,
and there the sterling cup, the silenced throat,
my twisting branches, rising, hold the wall.
In this garden, the one I know so well,
I am asleep in brackish dreams of hell.

June

Ode to the Rose (Centaurus)

In the flower shoppe,
the peeling red roses—
startling of love
from barrels in corners—
asking for respite in desperate voices,
writing on note cards in spidery scrawl
the quiet to steal heart after heart;
a subtle perfume, dense and aromatic,
as you were, the colourful bouquet,
woven dexterous
by angels.

The dark comes at the end of each evening,
blotting out the transgression of former hours,
piercing through our sin are the stars.
They compared me once to a night without stars.
In all her journeys into the soul,
a woman gathers her power,
as nature recreates itself each day.
Summoning all that is within her,
she imparts strength to those she loves
and those she must forgive,
writing them notes with flowers.

Ode to the Honeysuckle

Weathered, my twining vine grows toward Elba,
my yellow woodbine attracts singing birds,
fragrant, my nostalgia hides in old tales
and my trumpet flower calls, potion first
as a paradise on warm summer scents:
to the bees, they drunken float in woodland
air, mystical and proud, evanescent.
She asks your pardon for the dripping wand
of sickening smell, the perfume calling,
arching shrubs are pure floral remedy
unto the weak, and the night winds stalling
to emerge, putting all to sleep. Circe's
staff is paired with tannins, shades of deep blue
are the goat-leaf's fruit: whimsical and true.

Elegy of the Oak

Voice One.

Under the icy branches of winter,
where the smooth margins of the leaves
spin tales, and the solstice sun
lights to white,
the fragrant bottles gleam
with silver lids along the window
of my bedroom.

Here the cotton is spun, far
across a field, once harvested by black hands.
And here the outline of the trees,
Ravensara Antiqua Stencil.

In a little while, lay me down
in a pavane for a dead child
under the oak tree beside the waters,
where the shallows play with lights from above,
where the music of the ancients still croons,
and there in a tree will call your little dove.

Here the light flutter of whimsical
constancy,
and the marcescence.
I am never far from you,
for you are my decorous brown home,
where the lobed leaves are my nest,
and my ivory tower, the cage
in which I am captured beside the sky.

Voice Two.

I have put weight on you
and you have held
until death where I also will find you.
There is a swing in this tree of mysteries.
There are children who hover here.
Secret doors and marvellous passageways
in your mind,
I have hidden within,
I have built.

There is no more sadness, no sorrow here
to crease your old and clay-formed brow,
the alabaster arches of your visage,
the crooks of your arm and depth of your breast.
The worries of life have left you a hollowed boat
in which I will sail.

Voice One.

Let me move on into eternity
and I will not forget you at once,
you will not disappear,
my memories will lapse into etchings
and engrave the very ground I lie beneath
with the fragments of the oak leaves.

Let me sing beneath the earth
behind the veil of consciousness
where I have lapsed into the melody
I once sang. I am more
alive than I have ever been,
I can hear the crickets calling,
I can hear Odin ringing
his bell.

Voice Two.

Acorn hair streams and trickles down
in lassitude, in multicoloured blue fire,
a coat over the back of the poor,
malnutrition
like rivers under the moon.
It has been there for centuries,
rumouring on in elegies
and now its bridge, abiding, decays.

See how the branches hang
over the water, ministering,
and how we are strong
when we are individual flowers
with lexicons;
plagued until you pull
the cart out of the mud.

July

Ode to the Water Lily

Writing the words on my own flaxen flesh
my fascia has turned apatite moon,
over the hearth where I placed white mesh
like an old tutu over broken stone,
where the façade of brazen brick lay cracked.
Intakes of memories haunted the dance,
there was no more sorrow in God-forsaked
shoes, they hung here, pink ribbons happenstance,
and every glimmer of beads belayed the song,
water lilies, I would remember the steps
and broken body would sway back along
the marked floor, where I still hum out the rest—
forgetting all else, all time until death:
I will collapse on the wood floor, a wreath.

Ode to the Holly

I gave my last green gloved hand to the night
where fountains were trickling in the garden
and saw you there, reaping the holly's light:
dark velvet hooked claw that reached for pardon,
cast upon from heaven with vestal rays
that illumined Christmas Eve in pale snow,
and as a hedge would, daring, bar the way.
The wind winnowed, cast the plump berries, crowned
the centerpiece of regeneration,
amidst white candles of the wintry nape,
for sanctity rises veneration
from its center, a neck from woolen cape.
Could this be the ear that wears your diamond;
waxwing serenity tables violence?

Letter from a Douglas Fir

Upon my return
to the island,
I will visit you once again,
and will take you in my arms
the way I used to.

I used to take you
for walks under the Douglas fir trees
on the old hill
before the sun would burn
behind the branches.

I used to sing to you
at any traffic light,
and melodically entrance
every woman with their own song.

Why I even remember singing
"Que Sera, Sera,"
to the minister's daughter
with blond ponytails,
when she came to stay
with you
down at our cottage by the sea.

I have been gone for
so long.
I guess I left you
and your mother
when you were still young.

I moved to Australia,
I joined the gay community;
I wrote you at times when I was most lonely.
I don't have to put on a happy face anymore.

I am a Douglas fir now with an ancient face.
The sea moves in and out,
she is quite transient,
with grey salt.
I run my fingers through my hair,
and it is quite grey too.

If I see you again,
perhaps the rain will wash away
years of pain,
years of torment,
and I will know you once more
the way a father should.

August

Dogwood Crest

Lulla-lu, there is a voice here.
Lullaby-lu, a child sighing,
the wind is crying,
the fairies hide, dear.

Lulla-lu tiny child,
you open your small hands,
your eyes are wider to lands.
Lullaby-lu, slumber mild.

Your basket swings under the dogwood tree,
the flowers open to cradle the new,
and beloved generations before you,
their fragrance encircles me.

You are a lamb in the peppermint,
wooly-girl, a docent to the gallery
of books, in a field encircled by trees,
the grass and herb leaves glint.

All are loved within this circle of trees,
sanctity is royal navy,
and marriage is fit for a lady,
redeemed to loyalties.

Lulla-lu, but rest in sleep,
now off to the lullaby world
said your mother's curls,
before the shadows creep,
before the branches weep.

Where I Found Her (Goldenrod)

I found her
in a woodland meadow,
crafting a piper's tune,
the village brushed and eyes apart,
we, Sir,
beleaguered and bled
injustice.

He was tall without a hunch,
the castle on the moor,
echoed in glass,
the cottage thatch and thrush,
a recall
to Notre Dame's vast naves.

In this meadow,
the goldenrod,
crackling underfoot,
the sky a stormy
chase of thunder . . .
She stands,
two immigrants
in sorrow at the task
of Scotland, shapely
in a coat of arms.

CHOCOLATE & HAZELNUTS (found poem)

This Nut Brown Ale
is truly one of a kind.
A mahogany, English-American
hand-crafted brown ale
that carries notes of chocolate
and roasted hazelnuts.
Ending with a light, dry finish.
A much loved legacy brew originally
from Black Oak Brewing Co.

The Shoe Tree

They say the heroin addicts
in this town
tied all these shoes together
by hand,
and threw them into the
branches of a tree.

There must have been
a hundred pairs
in a large elm
full of shoes,
each one speaking of someone
without shoes.

Your name was Friday.
You were sitting in the
doorway when I found you,
you had walked a long way,
and your shoes were
dusty and torn,
the tongues gaping wide
over your bare feet.

There was a thought
that someone should buy
you another pair,
and should that
someone be me?

You were a lost boy,
and I was a shoe tree,
waving my arms,
insisting there are lots of shoes
for everyone.

September

Ode to the Aster (Columba)

If I had a house,
I would grow the purple morning glory
in profusion along the white picket fence,
bearing blooms
like the saucers of teacups,
holding the steaming aster,
profiting from the wake of dreams
like the foam oft the sea-born shore,
lashing its May night salvia
in a tumbling low vibrato of selves;
the wind, rippling her sleeves in operatic earnest.

I introduced the afternoon
to its late slanting rays
warming the grass and cooling the shade.
Divided between hot clasps and sipping cold ices,
the visitors would draw lots
to play croquet
with red, blue, and green mallets,
breathing impassioned circles
across the construed terrain,
a seasonable game
with varied opportune endings.

Winding Road

The fury of life
is depicted in its fortes,
unleashed by its powers,
drawn up from within—
while others hesitate
you roar from the desert,
kinetic eyes staring into the sun,
mimetic at an oasis of finery.

The wallpaper climbed like a vine,
and you were its flower;
in iris hues, warm and delicate,
you rebirthed prestige
from within a silver frame,
wore each bud,
and named each child
after you.

Marron (Ode to the Chestnut)

When standing, she is here in the dark night.
There is a shadow across the terrace—
the majestic form of a woman. Light
of the moon streaming through, her brave branches

reach to my windows, leafy, serrated.
Eyelet, my chestnut, in high curtained eyes—
spiny bur, lost after you fall, effaced
to the ground in autumn, with future ties

to your roots invisible. Second smell,
of the wheat—beyond the landscape—golden,
the place I grieve my broken nutshell,
the parting of my daughter—dance molten

to another tree. In enameled mind,
the pen of my perceptual poet
scrawls ink; to this heavy timber, the mine
where all directions cross and wrote.

At the rope-wreathed, linen-green matriarchs—
tulip-surrounded, standing in a line:
perpetual order usurps chaos
and blight, where they chant the prophetic signs.

Beyond distortions, shedding unnamed fear,
forest where the deer culminate unseen,
and every raindrop sheds marble tears,
we forge a common destiny with dreams.

October

Ode to an Arbutus

Peeling, a leper dressed in red,
the papery bark curls
reveal the olive bed
from which they sprang:
a plethora
of golden contrasts.
A polite green velvet glove
hand clasp,
the sea whispers azure
to the shore,
the wind whimpers
in its roar, along
Arbutus Road while its foam
disperses over the grey sand,
amid seagulls,
wallowing over the land.

Here the driftwood
is as an ancient face—
the bladderwrack is tea-stained lace.
Unmoving, silent, onward,
filtering bright,
the tree climbs toward
morning.

The sun is hot-white
with blue highlights,
while drying the peels
of a red tree's quarantined detritus.
Overhanging the sea,
its boughs drape
the water's edge,
the disguised shore
of Vancouver Island.

The long strips
are like paper,
parchment already
scrolled
for an academic
winter,
ensnared in the
wood street,
marked
by the contrast of branches
on fog.

I meandered in the mist
down the long winding roads
of this sunlit city
in a straw hat—
like porcelain,
my neck embellished
by a crocheted collar
bought at a
Garage Sale.

Where pear blossoms fall
littering the ground,
with its dulcet
civic spires
and wood heritage dwellings
with paned windows like eyes,
flower boxes,
peeling painted rocking chairs,
and stone mantelpieces.

Where hermits could live
in Beacon Hill Park
there is an old Fort Camosun,
still rising strong and true
amid the refuse of Victoria.

Stagnant,
they are as old water
running to Arbutus Cove
under the branches of the sea,
staving off the autumn
with stricken hands
covered in leprosy.

He was disguised,
disfigured,
stricken as if by plague,
driven out,
and quarantined in
Egypt for one year.
The bodies of his
civilians left
small craniums
the size of lily of the valley.

His love is a tree
over the water
unto his followers,
dying and groaning
and dying again. . .

Olde English Ode

Ivy, my sweet,
come dance with me—
into a space,
in frozen lace,
with your green eyes.

Ivy, my love,
come be my dove—
into the sky,
with your fine wings,
and your delicate beak.

Ivy, my dear,
don't shed a tear—
climbing the walls,
winding the stair.

Ivy my woman,
soon it will be summer—
and you will rise,
under the plum tree,
golden and free.

Ivy, my widow,
when you will weep—
with your arms flailing,
with your vines trailing. . .

Ivy, my life,
when you will lie
under the snow—
let the wind speak, darling,
let the wind blow.

November

Ode to the Spruce

Beside the sun's still dying light,
is the bleeding of the night.
The ink of darkness
fills the sky, illuminated
by stars alight in starkness.

With the traipsing spruce serene
of early boreal winter,
November's gems gleam
for the setting's spinster.

Beside the whorled branches low,
and over the hill's brow,
the soft needles borrow
from her mother's sewing basket.

In this time,
the left-over fragrance of frosty mornings,
and dry crisp afternoons
rose with the night. . .

The ocean before us,
rife with life,
as this line of spruce will tell,
witnesses to linen shells,
mollusks, crabs, and barnacles,
curated in tide pools
like seed wings.

O spruce, with nuances of green and gold,
has broken every metal mold,
you rise the ancient of the earth,
and here, your song still stings.

Cremated, our brittle bones,
are buried 'neath your fragile cones.
Our gifts beneath the tree
were wrapped in glitter and with bows.

Botanical imprints line the walls
of our sea cottage with wicker chairs.
The shape of your character
leaves a botanical imprint on my mind.

There is no one with quite such
windy boughs,
who is ever pink-cheeked
and never sallow as dripping wax pools
beneath my wood candlesticks.

There is no one with quite such
height against the night,
as to collect friends as well as enemies,
as the finds of a glass blower's moon.

The snow falls lightly
with an ice-cold rigour,
glossing on its sheen and
diluting the ever-green.

Ode to the Reed

There is a broken reed, a crumbled tow'r
that lies far beyond and oceans beside. . .
and framing inward dust in stone lower
than descant, the grey rocks lie round, reside
without shape, in deep darkness, without form,
and no longer anyone lives within.
There was once a pauper who with his page torn,
with his dank pen wrote of such rancid ruins,
but lately he stares out to the marine
grey tide, with old forgotten impetus
standing between him and his dream sublime.
Spilled goblets, and the wall in deference
to success, with time, decomposes, tainted.
Here the corpse is castle-scattered remains.

December

Elderberry Wine

When lightning strikes the elder tree,
come near my love, come near to me.
When elder wood shall play a flute
beneath the shadows of her station,
drawing near your fairy root,
heal our vows' regeneration,
with eternity's perfume.

When winter's solstice fills our dreams,
we plant you pale beside the back door,
protect us from enchantment's gleam,
and wind your branches 'round the floor.
Fashion from your wood a cradle,
make our future home be stable,
and forgive the child's lament.

Elderberries bring forth juice,
dripping from a poisonous tree,
with it we shall age our wine,
oaked and assay-mellowed,
husky, smooth, by expert winemakers.
All these trees stood in a field,
now berry nose, and with deep flavour.

Elderflower take my pen,
writing on this crystal gem,
your spray will fall into my glen,
floral, creamy, Summery.
And from your new stalk risen then,
from flow'rs shall your berries unfold,
and speak of when the earth was old.

When highlights form upon your branches,
leaves in the twilight's prosperity,
or we are sickened by the elderflowers,
under a blood moon's returning,
from a witch's potion—bitter flavour:
never scented musty or damp—
but, if they do, try heady smelling blooms.

The furrowed
crust of your grey-brown bark
with criss-crossed ridges, has groves
and lenticels like warts,
corky as my forehead,
home of seven larks,
adorns a compound of seven leaflets.

In scrub and hedgerows,
the site of cawing crows,
on railway embankments rue,
this short-lived cordial sweet
is identified by its scent and blossoming tree,
foraged in the springtime dew,
as a never ending cycle.

Mysterious tree of portals,
able to sprout anew
from seemingly dead wood,
you are called the "Tree of Life," and an amulet
of your blue wood
should be made to protect those who die,
or those who are afraid in the night.

I hang your leaves upon my windows,
I protect my children from the dark of winter,
I bless the ill-timed with your oil,
I find your opportunity inert,
you are grown around a dairy, and your wine
   never spoils.
If only your fragrance could fall like rain
into the hard wood of my heart.

The floral essence has a long history,
of bringing delightful vigour
and relieving misery.
Even if the child died, and in death,
while your knitting needles purled—
as for deep grief, opening
one's eyes to the magic of the world.

Requiem for Bear Manor

Where the dogwood tree's shade casts last shadows
and the wind from the wood through the branches
of time winds its way across the blue manse,
here, pools of inward fancy are shallows,
veins curving distinctively in untoothed leaves.
Large white petal-like bracts composed a mind
for the botanical nuances, signs
of celestial appearings, dark speech
from realms beyond the cloudless pewter sky.
At this one pulpit I alone would stand,
preacher of secrets held within a God,
the breeze Nantucket, dress blue striped and dyed,
and orator of whisperings of lands:
where singular speaker outdid the mob.

Hinting of the moments of sunshine bright
I stood apart listless, pale like a moon,
I breathed of air far above clouds and crooned
while playing my guitar of broken light
streaming through famous panes on afternoons
with shadows hiding under wood antiques,
and strumming of new song and chords oblique,
when lentils simmered, the stove ladled soup.
I saw a glimmer of hope in lyrics
that wore sundresses, with lip gloss tinted,
where the bedraggled look melded away,
and our singing was observed by clerics
dressed in dark suits and starched collars minted,
the dead were carried to funeral bay.

The parting hand clasp of the deeper sea,
as she spit on shore the killer whale—black—
who had passed and was mourned in a large stack
of bulletins with tide's finality.
There was the figure here now dressed with sand,
who in coral sea star found her earring,
and with culprit sage seaweed blistering,
decayed beneath the heat upon the land.
This body wreathed with torment there would lie,
where bitterness was gathered 'neath her breast
departed, there horizon would vacant
stare, unhindered at beautified sunrise.
Her once maternal sentiment and breath
had soothed the hungry untimely vagrant.

Without the home of the oceanic
temple, deep water could not be broken
top to bottom, and if wine-like token
paired with marine's illusive sacrament.
Loitering crabs now would scatter beneath
ruined masts and shipwrecks of galleons
from medieval drime, pea sheen of bullions
in lorish trunks that once shone with god speak.
Flashing aqua fins of silver mermen
were like lush music in velveteen sea,
where pearl illusive crowns with wisdom's down
as swans upon the salt of hard sternum
of a mortal dowager's frosty tea,
premeditated wrath bequeaths her frown.

Heaven drawing close with finality,
feather'd angelic host peered 'round the door,
while hell slammed shut the bottom bunker poor,
they strummed with brass congeniality.
No music rivaled this one strain on earth,
for its equal none could eloquent sing,
nor dine without the meringue recipe
that was featured in flute-like hall of mirth.
Champagne be then poured for one and our pearls,
we would bow our heads at graced royalty,
among reed grass—the winsome laughter rings,
chocolate mousse, topped with chocolate curls—
that from the mermaid is glass loyalty,
among the elite of heaven, they sing.

At this poor pot, the peppermint reaches
from the shadows to the light of the sun,
it dilates its veins to climb and running
from morning to evening, dark green stretches.
From this lesson, our orator took note,
whereby she often listened to Jason,
placed the bust of Medea, she wrote him,
with blue and green lines floating from her boat.
What verse and of what pow'r shall I be best
visited? she asked. Frequented, she was,
by supernal beings, heard poetry
from afar, and it was fleeting soul rest,
yet she longed for the divine as tall mast,
on this ebullient ship lucidly.

The textured isle of power she now lived on
was rough to the touch, and her skin was smooth
and resinous with milky and opaque roots
in former times. For here was the dream long
into the night, the place where running drummed
and met the pavement, every house, dark-limp
an audience to her sounding trumpet.
She hit the mark, star shone and illumined—
with one round white gleam that was her flashlight—
the stark dead, for she travelled there alone
and she exhaled the truth in bitter moans.
A warrior now at battleground to fight,
birthpains of Christ within her feet were stone,
and in her wrecked palms, the wretched nail holes.

Ishii Weeping

The mimosa tree is a delightful spectacle
of bright pink flowers.

Stranded in the fiery sky of desert,
rising over the ghosts of black Africa
she is fragrance of a khaki army,
and the reigns of a horse.
I am only a child.

The delicate pink blooms resemble starbursts and
grow during the summers in small clusters.

She will not give up—
her ambient will is strong;
she is aromatic, resistant to yellow drought
and tolerates low rainfall.
Let me tell you the story on parchment
of our Mimosa in the clinic compound
that day, as I remember it.
The nurse stroked my head
with Jojoba oil and
and gave me a bar of black soap
from the ash of a green plantain peel.

However, do not be deceived
by their appearance, as
they are hopelessly short-lived . . .

She came to us
both beautiful and deadly
with her belly swollen
and ready to burst.
I had been abandoned by my mother
and stood half hidden in the doorway,
the shade mingling with my
short reddish hair and
dark skin, luminous sebum.

The fragrant pink threads of flowers
and the sweet nectar attract hummingbirds,
honeybees, and butterflies,
which creates a beautiful wildlife scene.

It was a stricken heartbeat
we heard from within
the sea of an invisible face,
coral bones, a tiny vertebrate skeleton
stretching from the Red Sea
to Madagascar in the South,
as if feeding African fishermen
with giant tiger prawn.
A rumble of voices came from
within as the doctor rushed out
to help Mimosa.

If you are considering growing
mimosa trees, you should know
everything about them
before bringing them home.

The hair of her baby was
as fine as zonaria in the tide's pull,
or the oyster thief, I swear to God.
I saw it myself (and I am only a child).

The Albizia julibrissin is the genus name
of the mimosa tree.

She cried out in pain
right there
in the compound
in the dust, in front of us,
her tenuous voice
dulling my ostrich egg eyes
of youth
without a flicker of shame,
swathed in mosquito netting
that surrounded her in birth
like the clean camphor shroud
of a eucalyptus,
where mothers were squatters
compared to the fine houses of the white.

Mimosa trees have a
priceless appearance.
However, horticulturists and gardeners
refer to them as "trash trees"
due to their numerous issues.

Mimosa had her coarse black hair
tied up in a foraged scarf,
Capulana, thick
and rife with Portuguese colour,
but it escaped against the ruinous amber sky
and the red of her blood mingled with
her black porous skin.

The mimosa is called the Persian silk tree.

That night the moon would rise, a half
true limpet shell
and now she slept under cool sterile sheets
of the clinic, cared for by the nurse
from California.
I—lying on my small cot,
just like I would drape myself in the arms of the
baobab—was silent.

Mimosa trees are fast-growing flowering
that may grow up to fifty-two feet.

I walked to the water cooler
at midnight.
I poured a glass of cold
mineral water.
There were two sets of
glimmering eyes
I saw in the dark,
like lions stalk their prey
in the dead of night.

The mimosa belongs
to the Fabaceae family.

The two women stared at each other in the
dim glow of the monitor;
the things they had in common were
their soft orange skin from
mangoes,
the running of feet,
innocence:
making pain and trauma
look effortless.

The mimosa's fern-like leaves resemble
the leaves of palm trees
and close at night or during the rainy season.

The nurse bound
the baby to her back
tightly
the next day,
in a printed cloth sling.
She walked the long,
journey home
of a decrepit mile, next to the rude sheep and goats,
under the hot round sun,
and the moon disappeared,
shaped like an avocado sliced
on a mango wood board.

The mimosa tree became popular for its
texture and for its stunning looks,
as its leaves provide
an aesthetic background
for the colourful silk-like flowers.

She named her ebony-black
baby girl, still struggling to breathe,
curled in a pelican's beak,
after the nurse called Della—
while the leaves of the mimosa
brushed her face—
she smelled like the baby-pink
fetal-hued clusters,
as oil rises into the atmosphere.

The mimosa trees bloom in the depths
of summer, when they are
adorned by lovely flowers
and roamed under in
the savannah woodlands by zebras.

Other Tree Poems

The young air saw us true,
fresh and fragrant
as the pale bloom,
which, watered by
the moon's still light,
held mirror of our tender trust
in every brush-drawn petal.

While feet were tender-bathed
in ribboned grass of healing green,
our love stole forth ...
as breath, in dewy stillness
of the morn
and watched the
sunrise fling its gold.

The pattering rains of spring
would come
and chafe us with their
cleansing tears,
then cease to pristine sweetness,
and our faces,
dampened,
shone their grace.

But friendship bound beneath
the supple trees,
once fragranced by their
line-traced leaves,
would, painted autumn's fire,
fall,
now muted, browned,
to dying ground—
as nature sheds her youth
for wiser things.

The acrid smoke of
fall remains
still burns the eyes
and mind,
its ashes scattered on
the wind.

The field is hard,
and colder grows,
as winter's white ice
claws its way across
the earth,
drawing unto death.
The darkness creeps,
and days, too long
and shadowed, chill.

Then fades the last
remaining light,
save for the glare of stars on snow,
as life is lulled to silent sleep
in frozen, well-numbed agony.

Yet I remain
beneath
this year-scarred tree
and wait,
in hope of spring.

The Wildings

Classic

Foliage and the violet orchards
flowered and picked,
the folded and faded variety:
preserving traditions
with old jam.

Fields of fruit,
from Kent to Cambridge, vigor—
a strawberry flavour, the most
English of all.

Linen Press

The pots, upside down
and brown
holding earth, as we
dry the moss and lichen,
a decorative accent.

The hot water
on the pot-bellied stove,
a twenty-minute endeavor:
the basins, for snow-pure
sheets, socks, and scarves
hanging in the breeze.

Inglenook

Castlehaven,
an engraved charcoal flight,
the ancient Romans
on the isle of wings:
the pigeonholes, laced
antique boots, leather-brown,
and monarchs converging
on wild asparagus.

The tiny white flowers
in a mother's apron:
freesia an ointment
from the 17th century onwards,
chimneys, a soot-tainted
handkerchief, and
a wreath over the door knocker.

Provencale

Pots and pans
in a quiet space,
small head, with one
moment's wish;
cloth towels to wipe away
smears, and a wild goose lake
where the blue stains.

Hand mirrors,
silver, ivory, and ebony,
with chaste and embossed
flowers: wreaths, ribbons, and bows;
in the hedge, small wildings
heckling the wrens.

The Gardener

The water can,
silver-blue and rain
falling into hay barrels;
the clouds, a thick lining
against Portugal's clavier.

An indent per daffodil,
and weather-worn ladder
for the garden shed,
white-washed
under a tangle.

Blackbirds, blossoms,
redwings, and fieldfares
join in after the frost.

Gloucestershire

Apples, no two alike,
from old cores,
grown among the verges.

Hidden deep in the woodland,
its seeds a jumble
for foxes, pies, and cider,
the crab apple dons its apron.

From pollen to blossom,
field to field:
woodpeckers, nuthatches,
and thrush nesting mistletoe
in the old apple wood.

Alabaster

Pondering through the boughs,
barrier to wind or stock,
the wildings
in the Welsh uplands,
pink with blossoms:
weighted down with
small green spheres,
the autumn, a hidden tryst
with light:
ripening a tune.

One apple for three thorns,
pips, as hedgerow root stock,
and graft a twig
from morn to moon.

Endnotes

Idyll of the Iris, p. 16. Emily Isaacson, republished from *Victoriana* (Potter's Press, 2015), 29.

Dreamscape Grey (Ode to the Ash), p.17. Emily Isaacson, republished from *Hallmark: Canada's 150 Year Anniversary* (Dove Christian Publishers, 2017), 49.

Ode to the Rose (Centaurus), re-named p.36. Emily Isaacson, republished from *A Familiar Shore* (Tate Publishing, 2015), 94.

Dogwood Crest, p.50. Emily Isaacson, republished from *Hallmark: Canada's 150 Year Anniversary* (Dove Christian Publishers, 2017), 4.

Where I Found Her (Goldenrod), p.52. Emily Isaacson, republished from *The Fleur-de-lis Vol III* (Tate Publishing, 2011), 151.

The Shoe Tree, p.54. Emily Isaacson, republished from *Love in the Time of Plague* (Potter's Press, 2022), 184.

Ode to the Aster (Columba), re-named p.58. Emily Isaacson, republished from *A Familiar Shore* (Tate Publishing, 2015),114.

Winding Road, p. 59. Emily Isaacson, republished from *Victoriana* (Potter's Press, 2015), 64.

Other Tree Poems ("III, IV"), p.89. Emily Isaacson, republished from *The Fleur-de-lis Vol III* (Tate Publishing, 2011), 283-285.

The Wildings p.92. Emily Isaacson, republished from *The Fleur-de-lis Vol III* (Tate Publishing, 2011), 75-82.